Spy in the Sky

Kathleen Karr

Illustrated by Thomas F. Yezerski

Hyperion Books for Children
New York

For Daniel
—K. K.

Text © 1997 by Kathleen Karr.
Illustrations © 1997 by Thomas F. Yezerski.

Printed in the United States of America.

First Edition

1 3 5 7 9 10 8 6 4 2

The artwork for each picture is prepared using pen and ink.

This book is set in 13-point Leawood Book.

Library of Congress Cataloging-in-Publication Data
Karr, Kathleen.
Spy in the sky / Kathleen Karr ; illustrated by Thomas Yezerski.—1st ed.
p.   cm.
Summary: When Northerner Thaddeus Lowe lands his huge balloon in South Carolina at the beginning of the Civil War, ten-year-old orphan Ridley Jones joins up with him and the two set out to find a way to use Lowe's balloon to help the North.
ISBN 0-7868-1165-X (pbk.)—ISBN 0-7868-2239-2 (lib. bdg.)
1. Lowe, T. S. C. (Thaddeus Sobieskie Coulincourt), 1832-1913—Juvenile Fiction. 2. United States—History—Civil War, 1861-1865—Aerial operations—Juvenile fiction. [1. Lowe, T. S. C. (Thaddeus Sobieskie Coulincourt), 1832-1913—Fiction. 2. United States—History—Civil War, 1861-1865—Aerial operations—Fiction. 3 Hot air balloons—Fiction. 4. Orphans—Fiction.] I. Yezerski, Thomas, ill. II. Title.
PZ7.K149Sp   1997
[Fic]—dc21   96-45073

Contents

One

It Came from the Sky

Balloons never land where you want them to.

It's a fact of life. And I learned it from Thaddeus Lowe. Balloons have a lot of hot air, too. That's another fact. But I already knew about hot air. I've been getting hot air from grown-ups for ten years. That's as long as I've been alive.

Being an orphan isn't easy. Being an orphan in the piney woods of South Carolina is plain hard.

Fetch this, Ridley. Fetch that. Draw some well water. Chop the wood. Ridley Jones, shake a leg! You're eating on my mercy. You're sleeping on my straw. It's my hand will whip you. Your mama in heaven left you for good and final.

"Yes, ma'am. No, ma'am. Right soon, ma'am."

That was South Carolina for me. And that's where I was on *the* day. The day that big balloon came floating through the sky. Musket balls were chasing it. That's because war just broke out. It was a war between the South and the North. But I didn't care one way or the other. I already lived through my piece of hard times. That balloon was coming out of heaven, where my mama was. It looked like better times to me right off.

It flew over the village. It almost stuck on the church steeple.

"Angels coming!" some people said.

Then a heavy bag fell. It came from the balloon's basket.

"Ain't angels coming!" said others.

2

The balloon rose a little higher.

"It's the devil. Dressed all in black!"

"It's a Yankee spy!"

Another bag fell. The balloon bobbed over the town square.

"He's come to bomb us! Aim your guns!"

"No!" I yelled. "That balloon's in trouble!"

"Hush up, Ridley Jones. Orphans got no cause to talk."

"But it's trying to land!"

No one paid me any mind, so I ran right over to where it drifted. I looked up. The man in the basket pulled at wires. Another bag fell.

"Need some help?" I called.

The man grabbed at his black cape. He leaned over the basket. His long black mustache drooped. "Where am I?" he shouted.

He hung lower now. Just above me.

"Ten feet over South Carolina. Come on down."

"But those shots . . ."

I shrugged. "Nothing to be scared of. The brave men are all gone to war. Only cowards left."

He swept the high silk hat from his head. He bowed. "Thaddeus Lowe, young man. Catch the anchor. I'm landing."

Turns out Mr. Lowe was testing the balloon. He came from the North. He'd been in the air for a week and didn't know about the war. I told him.

"Bad timing." He caught some balloon cloth.

"Sure is." I caught some more.

We stuffed it into bags. No one else helped. They were still pointing their guns. They still thought he was a Yankee spy. But they didn't shoot.

"How do I get back North, Ridley Jones?"

"Railroad, I guess. It's still running."

"How do I find the train?"

I kept stuffing. "Reckon I could show you.

You need the help."

I stopped. I looked at him again. He was the most interesting man.

"Reckon you need help all the way North."

He pulled at his black cape like he was cold. He did have a skinny, long body. But it was April. Not that cold. He stared at the guns. "A helper might be good. What of your mother and father?"

"Don't have any."

Mr. Lowe looked at my ragged clothes. He took in my yellow hair and blue eyes. "Have you got curiosity?"

I grinned. "Enough to kill a cat."

He bowed a second time. "Lead the way, young man."

That's how I got to be helper to Thaddeus Lowe, the famous balloonist.

Two

Taken for Spies

Nobody cried when I left. Nobody even noticed.

They sure were glad to see the back of Thaddeus Lowe, though. They were so glad, they fixed him up with a wagon. He wouldn't go without his balloon things. It took eight mules to get it all to Unionville. That's where the trains came through.

Night got to Unionville before we did. Maybe that's why they took us to the jail first. A possible spy seemed scarier to them in full black night, I guess. I didn't much like the idea of jail. It was sure to have dirty straw.

Worse than what I always slept on.

The talk got loud in front of the jail. It got a little nasty. It was time for some of that help I was meant to give.

I slipped off the cart and snuck behind the jailhouse. I took a deep breath and let out a howl.

"Whooo—ahhh!"

Like to devils and ghosts it was. It sounded fine. The voices in front went quiet. I gave it another try.

"Whooo—ahhh—ooog!"

Then I dressed it up some.

"Whooo . . . send him a-way . . . far a-way. . . ."

That seemed enough. I trotted back again. The jailer was already locked behind his doors. The balloon and basket were tossed on the ground. The mule team was halfway home.

Mr. Lowe and I spent the night in a hotel. It was my first hotel. Not a blade of straw anywhere. Right nice.

* * *

The morning train took us to Columbia. It was the biggest place I'd ever seen. It was my first train ride, too. But more trouble was waiting.

Maybe word traveled ahead from Unionville. Maybe that big pile of balloon things standing next to us on the platform did it. Pretty soon, along marched a whole troop of soldiers. They took us for spies, too. We stared into their gun barrels. We stared into their eyes. These soldiers were no cowards. Next thing, we're in a big building, talking to some generals. Mr. Lowe was not happy.

"Look here, gentlemen," he said. "My papers." He pulled them from his coat. He slapped them on the desk.

"I am not a Yankee spy. I am a scientist of the air. I study which way the wind blows. I have just found an east wind that will take me across the ocean. It brought me to South

Carolina first." He stopped, looking a little sad. His mustache drooped. "Balloons never land where you want them to."

All those generals listened. They read his papers. Then they pointed at me. I was standing behind Mr. Lowe. I was trying not to be seen. Columbia was bound to have a bigger jail than Unionville. It was bound to be meaner, too.

"Who's that?"

Mr. Lowe turned with a swoop of his cape. "This," he said, "is my assistant."

I stood taller. *Assistant* was a much bigger word than *helper.* Fancier, too.

Those generals laughed.

That put me out some. But it also put them in a good mood. *I* made Thaddeus Lowe look harmless. The generals wrote out a new paper for him. They stamped it with wax. Turns out it was a passport to the North. We left fast.

Outside, Mr. Lowe looked me over again.

"It worked in there," he said, "but it might not work on the train North. We must get you some new clothes, Ridley."

Somebody was going to give me something *new*?

Well, Mr. Lowe did. They were fine new clothes. Wasn't a hole anywhere. It took some doing setting my feet in boots, though. I'd been barefoot all my life. I limped all the way back to the train. I gritted my teeth and did it for Mr. Lowe.

The train was very long. It was filled with very quiet people. They were so quiet, we took them for Northerners. Northerners not looking for trouble. Thaddeus Lowe and I settled in.

It took four days to get North. Along the way, Mr. Lowe tried to find how much learning I had.

"Can you read, Ridley?"

"Well, yes, sir. I guess I can. All those

widows I lived with? They taught me so's I could read the good book. It passes the time on a winter's night."

"Can you do arithmetic?"

"You mean counting? I can count on my fingers fine." I held up my hands. "See here? Ten fingers. Add 'em up."

He pulled away a hand. "How many left?"

"Five. Any fool can see that!"

He smiled. His mustache curled. "It's a start. But we'll have to do better if you truly want to help with my work."

"I do!"

So Mr. Lowe, he pulled some paper from his carpetbag. He began covering that paper with numbers. Little drawings, too. Soon the paper was dancing with tiny balloons. I learned it took more than hot air to make one rise. It took numbers, too. Without numbers you couldn't figure the right amount of gas to use.

The first day flew by. Every so often, we'd

look out the window. Southern soldiers were gathering all along the tracks. I started in counting them, for practice. Next I counted their tents. When I got past hundreds, I learned how to write down the numbers. That's what got us into trouble again.

It was near the end of the day. The train stopped at a station. It was swarming with soldiers, and a big one came into our car.

"I am Major Todd of the Confederate States of America!"

He let us know right off. He was that proud of his shiny new uniform. Then he started in giving a speech. Outside, a brass band was playing. I thought I knew the song. But it was hard to tell for sure. There were a lot of wrong notes. I held my ears against the noise. Major Todd noticed. He stopped his speech, which was all about being true to the South.

"You, there!"

My hands dropped. "Me, sir?"

"Are you not a true Southerner?"

"Born in South Carolina, sir."

He stomped closer. "Why were your ears covered?"

"Earache, sir. From the drafty train . . ."

"Papers!" he roared.

Mr. Lowe pulled out our papers. But Major Todd saw our number sheets first. He grabbed them. "I knew it! Spies! Counting our troops! Yankee spies! The whole train is filled with them!"

"That's just my lessons, sir . . ."

Well, it took a heap of talk before Mr. Lowe got us out of that one. The other people went stone scared, too. At last the band outside stopped playing. The train began to move. Major Todd was not happy. But he gave back our papers.

"If they were not signed by a general . . . you'd be hanged!"

He jumped off the train. That was the end of our written lessons.

* * *

Three long days later we got to Kentucky. We collected the balloon and went to the river. A ferry was waiting to take us across the wide Ohio. On the other side was Cincinnati and the North.

That whole trainload of people got into the ferryboat with us. They were as still and silent as a tomb. As we neared the far side of the water, Thaddeus Lowe saw the huge flag first. It was flying from the docks.

"Look!" he shouted. "It's the Stars and Stripes!"

Well, you never heard such a ruckus. Near every soul on that ferry started in cheering. Round after round of cheers rose up to the sky. Like one of Mr. Lowe's balloons. I thought for only a moment, What had the South ever done for me?

I started in cheering, too.

Three

Dinner with Mr. Lincoln

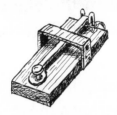

We didn't stay long in Cincinnati. Mr. Lowe got an idea in his head. He was a great one for ideas. And more stubborn than any mule about them.

"Ridley," he said. "Crossing the Atlantic Ocean can wait. The war is more important. Our balloons can help."

I liked the way he said that. *Our* balloons. I also thought about the folks back in South Carolina. The way they'd felt about his falling sandbags. "How, sir? For bombing?"

"Never!" The idea truly upset him. "Balloons are too pure for that. Like birds of

17

the air! But they *can* be used for defense . . ."

Well, he went into a lot of detail. But it all came down to one thing. He'd use his balloons to watch the enemy's troops. See what they were up to. Give any news to our troops.

"How?" I asked again.

He smiled. "That's where you come in, Ridley. I've bought you a present."

"Another present? After all those clothes?"

"Yes!" He thrust an object into my hands.

I looked at the strange thing. "What is it, sir?"

"It's a *key*. To tap out the Morse code. We will relay messages from our balloons, Ridley. Messages that can be sent by telegraph. We only have to convince President Lincoln. He's a wise man. He'll see the future. We leave for Washington City tomorrow."

"Fine by me." I started packing.

* * *

Thaddeus Lowe was the best teacher. Never wasted a minute, either. All the way to Washington City by train he was teaching me.

I learned the Morse code. The code was a way of sending messages over wires by sound. There were only two sounds. There was the *dit* sound. Then there was the *dah* sound. Put together, they made letters. The letters made words. It was the most amazing thing. I took to it right off.

"Listen here, Mr. Lowe." The train was chugging through Pennsylvania. The view was nice. But my Morse code key was nicer. I'd had it on my lap for hours. Tapping, then tapping some more. I went at it again.

Dit-dit-dit . . . dah-dah-dah . . . dit-dit-dit.

"Know what that means?"

"SOS." His mustache curled. "The danger signal."

"Yes, sir. I can't wait to get up in that balloon!"

"Patience, Ridley. First we must talk to Mr. Lincoln."

19

* * *

Washington City was more like a big town than a city. It had dusty streets. And more soldiers than I'd counted coming all the way North. Only these were dressed in blue instead of gray. But that huge old Capitol building was something. So was the White House. Like a palace, it was. And why not? President Abraham Lincoln was a big man. He deserved a big house.

Washington City had a castle, too. Made of red brick, with towers and all. It was called the Smithsonian. That's where we put our balloon things. On account of that's where smart people worked. *Scientists.* People with big ideas like Mr. Lowe. I loved those big ideas. Someday I would be a scientist, too. I already knew it in my bones.

Mr. Lowe and I stayed at the best hotel. The Willard Hotel. It was near as spit to the White House. It was filled with important men. From the size of their cigars, they had to be.

Mr. Lowe sent lots of telegrams to Mr. Lincoln. Then we waited for an answer. While we waited, we went down to the park around the Smithsonian. We practiced with his little balloons. I learned how to fill them with gas. I learned how to send them up to the heavens.

Thaddeus Lowe kept me running. But it was different from chopping wood. Different from drawing well water. I think my head grew three sizes from all the learning.

Mr. Lowe was trimming his mustache when the message came. A knock on the hotel room door. I opened it.

"Telegram for Thaddeus Lowe."

Mr. Lowe tossed me a nickel. "Sign for it, Ridley."

I signed for it. I gave the tip. I waited for Mr. Lowe to read it. He whooped.

"Greetings from President Lincoln! My ideas interest him. And could we join him for dinner tonight?"

21

I whooped, too. Thaddeus Lowe always started at the top.

That night I wore my Sunday shirt. My boots were polished. My pants were pressed, too. Mr. Lowe wore his black cape and his tall silk hat, like President Lincoln's. We could have walked to the White House easy, but Mr. Lowe hired a carriage.

"Style, Ridley. Sometimes you have to wrap up your package with a little style."

So we arrived in style. Us and a few things for proving ourselves. Mr. Lincoln was waiting in a huge room inside. The room sort of matched his size. He shook hands with Mr. Lowe. Next, he shook my hand and smiled. Then he turned to a servant.

"Ask Willy to join us for dinner, please. This might interest him."

I wondered who Willy might be. Mr. Lowe just started in on his speech. Pretty soon I found out about Willy. He was a boy about my age. President Lincoln's son! He was friendly, too. It came to me that I hadn't played with another boy in a coon's age.

"Hey," I said.

"Hey," he answered.

"Want to see something great?"

"Wouldn't mind."

So we left the president and Mr. Lowe talking away. Willy and I took those things we'd brought. We walked right out of the room through some windows. Like doors they were. Right onto the lawn outside. I opened the first box. I took out a little gas machine. "How's your arithmetic?" I asked.

Willy liked those baby balloons fine.

"See?" I told him after we had one in the air. "This is how our balloons will work. They'll rise up with a basket. But they won't fly free. We'll connect a telegraph line to the basket. I'll be up there tapping back messages. I'll see the whole battlefield below. I'll

see *everything*—nearly to forever!"

"Gosh," Willy said. "You think my pa would let me go up, too? I'd really like that!"

"You know the Morse code? There's no room for slackers up there!"

"I'll learn!"

The sun was starting to set. The little balloon was real pretty, floating up there. It was all pink and red. Willy wanted to hold the ropes. I let him.

"Pa!" he yelled. "Hey, Pa!"

"What is it, son?"

I turned around. There was Mr. Lincoln, standing outside the house. He was way tall. But our balloon was taller. He saw it in the sunset.

"Look here, Pa! Ridley and I sent up this balloon ourselves!"

"It's no trouble," I added.

"Think of a huge balloon, Pa," Willy said. "Think of it floating like a cloud. Right over an enemy battlefield."

"Think of a body up there, sending down messages," I went on. "By telegraph line. You'd know exactly what was going on, sir. Easy as pie."

President Lincoln turned to Mr. Lowe. "This is more than a circus, isn't it, Mr. Lowe."

Thaddeus Lowe let out his breath. "Yes, Mr. President. Balloons are not just for showmen. They can also be helpful in war."

Mr. Lincoln turned to us again. "Come in for your dinner, boys. We have a lot of plans to make. About a Balloon Corps."

Four

Can It Be Done?

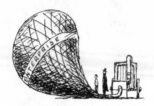

What's to become of our project, Ridley?"

Poor Mr. Lowe was yanking at his mustache something fierce. He did that when he was upset. He'd like to pull it out one of these days, if things didn't start to move along. The Balloon Corps wasn't moving. And it was all on account of that old General Scott.

"How old you say General Scott is, sir?"

"*Old*, Ridley. This is 1861. General Winfield Scott's so old, he was the hero of the Mexican War in the forties. He's so old, he was the hero of the War of 1812!"

I whistled. "That's sure *old*. I never even heard tell of those wars."

Mr. Lowe swept them away with his long arms. "No matter. It's *this* war we need to win now. And Scott can't see the future. He can't think of a balloon as an *airship*."

"Mr. Lincoln's letter didn't help? He's the commander in chief!"

Mr. Lowe shook his head and sighed. "General Scott wants to do things his way. We'll have to prove ourselves again, Ridley."

How we got to prove ourselves again was almost fun. First off, we snuck behind General Scott's back. We went straight to officers in the field. They mostly thought balloons were a great idea. Of course, they wanted to see one in action. Mr. Lowe and I, we figured that made sense.

It was midsummer already. The weather was perfect for balloons. So one day we prepared the *Enterprise.* That was the name Mr.

Lowe gave his balloon that found me in South Carolina. We blew her up. We tied her to a wagon and brought the *Enterprise* across the river to Virginia. I was excited. Virginia was enemy country.

Some of our soldiers were waiting. They were worried. There weren't enough Northern pickets—that's what they called guards—around to protect us. Turns out our balloon was lucky. Those Southern troops saw this monster bobbing toward them. What did they do? They ran!

Well, of course I was itching to get up in that balloon. All this time I'd been learning about balloons. All this time I'd been studying my Morse code. I figured I was *ready*. I also figured I deserved it. The officers thought different. *They* wanted a ride!

So there I was, stuck on the ground. Mr. Lowe went up with one man at a time. They all came down excited.

"You can see for fifty miles!" said one.

"I made a map!" bragged another. "It must be the first map from the sky!"

"We'll have it all over those Rebels!" yelled a third.

"Tell General Scott," begged Thaddeus Lowe. "Better yet, tell President Lincoln. Please."

Meanwhile, the war was moving along. Word came to Washington City that the enemy was but twenty-odd miles away. Our soldiers went out to meet the South. It was at a place called Manassas, by a stream called Bull Run. Lots of Washington people drove out in their carriages to watch the battle. They took picnic baskets. They were looking for a thrill. Mr. Lowe and I, we waited at the hotel. We were upset about not having balloons out there to help. Also, we neither of us had any stomach for the fight.

Turns out neither did all those Washington City people. They came back green and sick. The Battle of Bull Run wasn't any picnic. We lost. We lost most awfully bad. Mr. Lincoln sent us another message the next day.

Mr. Lowe and I went back to the White House. President Lincoln was waiting. He looked tired to the bone.

"I understand General Scott does not approve of a Balloon Corps, Mr. Lowe."

"No, sir, he does not."

The president picked up his tall hat. "Let us go and see about that."

I snuck a look around for Willy Lincoln, but he wasn't about. So, just like that, Mr. Lowe and I went for a walk with the president.

Soldiers were leaning about, all over the War Department. When they saw the president, they shaped up right quick.

"General Scott, please," President Lincoln said.

"He's, uh, *busy*, sir."

"So am I!" snapped Mr. Lincoln.

The soldier in charge looked unhappy. "He's taking a nap, sir."

"Wake him up!"

General Scott got woken up fast. He was patting at his gray hair when we walked in. He wobbled to his feet.

"It's a great honor, sir—"

"Stuff and nonsense, Winfield! I want to know why I haven't got a Balloon Corps yet. If we'd had a balloon over Bull Run, we might have won!"

General Scott gulped. "Mr. President—"

"Enough!" Mr. Lincoln turned to us. "You've met Thaddeus Lowe. This is his assistant. They know their business. I want a Balloon Corps today. And I want Mr. Lowe to be its chief!"

I paid no mind to the rest of the talk. President Lincoln himself had called me Mr. Lowe's *assistant*. President Lincoln himself had said I knew my business. I didn't care about the details. We had our Balloon Corps at last! I floated out of there as high as any balloon.

Five

Dressed for Action

Uniforms are sure nice. Of course, there's all kinds of uniforms. That's something else I learned while Mr. Lowe and I were still setting up the Balloon Corps.

That mess at Bull Run got us started, like I already said. But it still wasn't any piece of cake. Even with folks in Washington City scared silly, the South would march on us. The Rebels were close enough to do it. And Washington City was noway ready to defend itself.

"We must take the *Enterprise* on a free flight, Ridley," Mr. Lowe said. "Right over the old battlefield area."

"To see what those Southern troops are doing?"

"Indeed."

We hadn't got help from the army yet. Not the twenty soldiers promised. Not even the free gas. Thaddeus Lowe got ready to take off anyway. When something had to be done, he did it.

Well, I begged and begged to go along. Mr. Lowe would have none of it.

"If something goes wrong, I may need help, Ridley. You're my assistant. Who else can I trust?"

That made me feel good again, sure enough. Then I stopped to think. "You get in trouble, how in the world can I help?"

"Can you drive a wagon, Ridley?"

"Hope to heaven. Should've learned something in those piney woods."

"Good. I might need to be rescued. Here's my plan."

He bent low, and I listened.

* * *

Come next morning, I helped Mr. Lowe go aloft. Right from the Smithsonian grounds. The *Enterprise* rose higher and higher till it was just a speck. Then it hit the special air Mr. Lowe had talked about. The currents that blew one way or the other. They flew him south across the Potomac River. Just like he'd planned.

I didn't waste any time. I jumped into the old covered wagon he'd rented. I headed for the bridge, me and the four-horse team. Lucky I had a pass from Mr. Lincoln himself to get across. I drove through the pickets to the other side. Then I was in Southern country. That's when I got to use my first uniform.

I laughed when I put it on. Funny kind of uniform, that. It was nothing but my old rags from South Carolina. Mr. Lowe, he figured on my Southern voice being a help. He also figured on me blending in with those rags. He wasn't half right.

I kept that balloon in my sights the whole day. Mr. Lowe, he was going up and down and up again. He was a proper spy this time.

It took some doing to keep him in view. Had to leave the rutted road lots of times. Had to roll over fields. Once I heard shots. I looked up. The balloon was being attacked. Mr. Lowe dropped a sandbag and rose.

I thought about it. Nobody knew which side he was on. Could be the North taking potshots just as easy as the South. Next time I'd see he carried the Stars and Stripes. 'Least only one side would be shooting, then.

Round about sunset I lost sight of Mr. Lowe over some woods. He'd come down at last. How to get him out was the problem. I headed for the woods. A farmhouse stood in the way. A farmhouse with a pack of barking dogs. Soon there was a pack of Southerners, too.

"Where you going, boy?"

A big farmer stood square in the road.

Like an old oak, he was. His rifle looked young enough, though.

I pulled up the reins. I thought fast. "Evening, sir. I'm from over to Fair Oaks? My pappy sent me for wood. Fixing to make us some charcoal, he is. Melt down our old plows for musket balls. Goin' to get us some Yankees, we are."

"A little late in the day, ain't it?"

"Took most of the day to get here. Had to go around Yankee pickets right and left. Figure I'll camp out. Head back when I've got my load."

"Fair enough." He stepped back. So did all his relatives. The dogs kept barking.

"Hush up, Blue!" He kicked at a hound. It hushed.

I set off into the woods. Got that wagon just inside, out of sight. Checked nobody was after me.

"Mr. Lowe? . . . Mr. Lowe!"

"Up here, Ridley."

Well, I was used to him being up. But up on top of a giant tree was something else. Had to chop down that tree to get the basket out. A few other trees, too. It took us half the night. Then we loaded up. We almost got past the farmhouse till that same hound started in.

"Hush up, Blue," I growled.

He hushed.

Mr. Lowe, he just curled up in his black cape. A few miles later he spoke.

"I believed I was a good judge of men. I judged right with you, Ridley."

I smiled in the dark. Not only was I his assistant. Now I was a *man.* My chest stretched so, those old rags near burst. "What happened, sir?"

"Gas leak. Some of those shots hit true. But my mission was worth it. The South just lost its advantage. They aren't heading for Washington City."

"Won't Mr. Lincoln be pleased!"

We drove that wagon back to Washington City with the news.

Well, there's uniforms. Then there's *uniforms.* I guess my old South Carolina rags don't really count. Least they didn't once I got my true uniform. A beauty, it was. It came in September of 1861. That's when Mr. Lowe finally got his Balloon Corps together.

We were resting at the Willard Hotel when the package came. Mr. Lowe did like to keep his secrets. He studied that box with this little smile on his face.

"Ridley?" he said.

"Yes, sir?" I set down my Morse code key. I'd been fiddling with it, just to keep in practice.

"This, I believe, is for you."

I'd learned not to question his presents anymore. I tore into the box.

"Well. *Well, now.*" First thing I pulled out was a pair of blue Union pants. I held them

43

up to me. They just matched the growing I'd done since South Carolina. Probably 'cause I'd been eating better than in my entire life.

I whistled. "That there's *some* yellow stripe down the legs!"

Thaddeus Lowe smiled. "It is."

Next thing I pulled out was the dark blue top. Fine wool it was, for the winter coming on.

"It's got brass buttons down its entire front!"

"It does that," Mr. Lowe agreed.

Finally—at the very bottom—the best was waiting. It was a cap with a brim, and a kind of squished top. That would have been fine enough. But nothing could be as fine as what was on its front. Sewn there good and solid, it was.

"A patch! The Balloon Corps patch!"

Mr. Lowe stroked his mustache with pleasure. "Can't have my Morse code specialist out of uniform, can I? Especially up in my balloons."

I near gave Mr. Lowe a hug, I was that pleased. I hopped around a little instead. Then I whooped. Had to let out *some* steam.

"Whoo—eee!"

"Indeed," Mr. Lowe said. "You're going to be a fine Billy Yank, Ridley Jones."

Six

Aloft at Last!

My new uniform was only the beginning. Pretty soon, Mr. Lowe was planning like crazy.

He started in building seven new balloons. He set up wagon crews. Fifty-men big, those crews were. They could get us inflated and up in the air in a few hours! There were wagons to carry our own gas. There was even a wagon just to carry telegraph wire. Five miles of it!

'Course, that was my department. And I was truly bursting to show my stuff. Then one day it all really happened.

We were camped out in Arlington. Right across the river from Washington City, that is. Mr. Lowe rubbed his hands together. He studied his very own Balloon Corps. His soldiers were all at the ready. Finally, he looked at me.

"Ridley Jones?"

"Yes, sir, Mr. Lowe." I snapped to attention right fast.

"You've been patient, young man."

"Yes, sir. I have." I couldn't but agree. I'd been so patient, I was about to bust. I *had* to get up in one of the balloons soon.

Thaddeus Lowe pulled at his mustache. Playfully. "Patience is *not* its only reward. Today you shall help me test our new balloon."

I shuffled my feet. "Now, sir?"

I could hardly look at the new balloon. I was afraid. Scared she might disappear before my eyes. But she didn't. The soldiers had her up by her three ropes. They'd been testing the pulleys. Making sure and certain they could bring her down on call.

"I wasn't taking any chances for your security, Ridley," Mr. Lowe said. "You are too valuable an assistant. But now everything is safe."

He turned to his crew and gave orders. The balloon was lowered from the sky. The basket bobbed gently to earth. Thaddeus Lowe turned back to me with a little bow.

"After you, young man."

Well, I didn't wait for a second invite. I scrambled into that basket so fast, I landed on my head. While I sorted out my arms and legs, the entire Balloon Corps was laughing. At me. 'Least it sure seemed that way. First I turned red. Next I settled my cap back on my head. The one with the balloon patch on it. Then I broke out laughing, too.

The men let out a cheer.

"Hip-hip-hooray! Hooray for Ridley!"

It was for *me* they were cheering. Ridley

Jones, the orphan from the piney woods.

I gave them a smart salute. Didn't matter if I was still red. Mr. Lowe, he'd already stepped in beside me. He gave a signal. Up we went.

At last.

And it *was* wonderful. Above the trees all red and golden. Above the river. Into the wide blue endless sky.

"How high we going, sir?"

"To the top, Ridley. A full mile."

I watched the river turn into a ribbon beneath us. "Are we on duty?"

"We are. We're testing the telegraph line, too." He took off his army hat and ruffled his hair. "Excuse me. *You* are testing the telegraph line."

I flew near as high as that balloon over our heads. I was that happy. Then I settled down some. Started to notice things. Like how smoothly we were rising. There was a little bit of wind. But it bobbed us gently. What it felt like was, well—

"Floating on a cloud!" I finally crowed. "We're floating on a cloud! Near up to heaven. Wouldn't my mama be proud!"

I took a deep breath and leaned over the side of the basket. I didn't want to stop rising. I wanted to fly up forever.

But those three ropes finally stopped us. You could see the balloon over our head fighting. It wanted to keep going, too. Who wouldn't?

Mr. Lowe tapped me on the shoulder. I shook the dreams from my head.

"Ready for work, Ridley?"

"Yes, sir!" I picked up my Morse code set. This time it was connected to a real telegraph line. Connected all the way to land a full mile below.

"Tell them what you see, Ridley."

I looked at the earth spread out below me and began tapping. I told them what I saw.

First sight of enemy. Brown earth forts . . . twenty miles due south. White tent camps . . . solid squares of soldiers every which way.

I stopped tapping and began to count. My fingers took over again.

Fifteen regiments near Falls Church.

I told the Balloon Corps waiting down below. Told the army officers. Told President Lincoln himself. It was me, Ridley Jones, who could do all that.

Thaddeus Lowe

Thaddeus Sobieskie Coulincourt Lowe (1832–1913) was born in New Hampshire before the time of airplanes. The idea of flying always fascinated him. At fifteen, he sent a cat aloft with a huge kite. He returned the cat to earth safely, but it never spoke to him again!

At eighteen, Thaddeus became the assistant to a traveling science lecturer. He began his experiments with hot-air balloons. By the time he was in his twenties, he was building the biggest balloon ever made. He intended to fly the *City of New York* across the Atlantic

Ocean to Europe. His picture and a picture of the balloon were printed in newspapers and magazines all over the United States. He was famous until the big balloon failed. Next, he built the *Enterprise* and tested it. That test landed him in South Carolina at the beginning of the Civil War.

Thaddeus Lowe's adventures from that point are told in this story. He really was a respected balloonist, or *aeronaut.* He really did begin the Balloon Corps for President Lincoln and the Union army—although Ridley Jones, his assistant, is fictional.

After the war, Mr. Lowe settled in California with his wife and ten children. He continued to invent such things as the first ice-making machine. Today, Mount Lowe in southern California is named after him.

I Spy

Thaddeus Lowe was able to spy a lot of things while floating up in the air in one of his balloons. See if you can spy the following things in this picture: a book, a boot, a chair, a plant, a pot, a television, a jar, and a hat. Circle the items when you find them.

What a Puzzle!

Use the following words and names having to do with the Civil War to answer the clues below, and then fill in the crossword puzzle: GEORGIA, ROBERT E. LEE, FREEDOM, VERMONT, GETTYSBURG, ULYSSES S. GRANT.

Down
1. _____ is the name of a Northern state.
2. The general of the Southern army was _____.
3. _____ is the name of a Southern state.

Across
4. A famous battle was held at _____.
5. The general of the Northern army was _____.
6. The slaves wanted _____.

Seeing is Believing!

Scenes of the Civil War were mostly recorded by artists. There were only a few photographers at the time of the war because the camera was a fairly new invention. Often the artists would change the scenes around a bit to create a more interesting picture. So it was sometimes difficult to know what really took place just by looking at a drawing or painting. Look closely at these two pictures. They might look the same, but there are seven differences. Find and circle the things that aren't the same.

Puzzle Answers

Just the Facts

1. T	7. T
2. F	8. T
3. F	9. F
4. T	10. T
5. F	11. F
6. T	12. T

Flying High

AERONAUT

I Spy

What a Puzzle

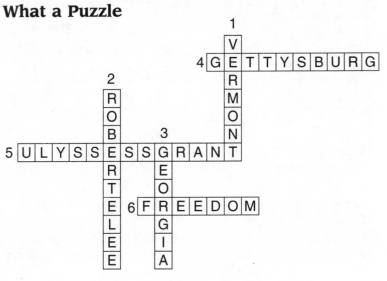

Seeing is Believing

Scene 1
1. one tree on street
2. building with 10 windows
3. sun and clouds
4. street light
5. full garbage can
6. no birds
7. solid awning on building

Scene 2
1. 2 trees on street
2. building with six windows
3. just clouds in sky
4. telephone pole instead
5. empty garbage can
6. birds flying though air
7. dotted awning on building